HOT CARS

FORD MUSTANG

CHARLES PIDDOCK

Guided Reading Level: T

rourkeeducationalmedia.com

Scan for Related Titles and Teacher Resources

TABLE OF CONTENTS

Planes, Horses, and Automobiles 4
New Look 9
American Muscle Car 10
Lee Iacocca's Baby 14
A Mustang Timeline 18
Lights, Camera, Mustang! 28

Getting Greener	29
Glossary	30
Index	31
Show What You Know	31
Websites to Visit	31
About The Author	32

HOT CARS   FORD MUSTANG

PLANES, HORSES, AND AUTOMOBILES

It was the terror of the skies during World War II (1939 – 1945). The Mustang P-51 fighter-bomber looked sleek and mean, like a giant wasp. It could sweep down from 15,000 feet (4,572 meters) and knock out anything on the ground or kill any enemy plane in the air. It became a legendary war machine. The P-51 took its name from the mustang, the wild horse of the U.S. West.

> The English word *mustang* comes from the 16th century Mexican-Spanish word *mestengo*, which means "an animal that strays."

HOT CARS   FORD MUSTANG

P-51 Mustangs fly in formation above the clouds.

The Ford Mustang car captures the **essence** of both the airplane and the wild horse. Put your foot on the pedal of a Ford Mustang and you feel one thing above everything else: power! The Mustang is designed to overwhelm the senses with its pulse-raising **torque** and the roar of its legendary engine.

John Najar, the designer of the first Mustang, supposedly named his design after the Mustang airplane. Lee Iococca, the Ford auto executive who developed the Mustang, says it was directly named after the wild horse.

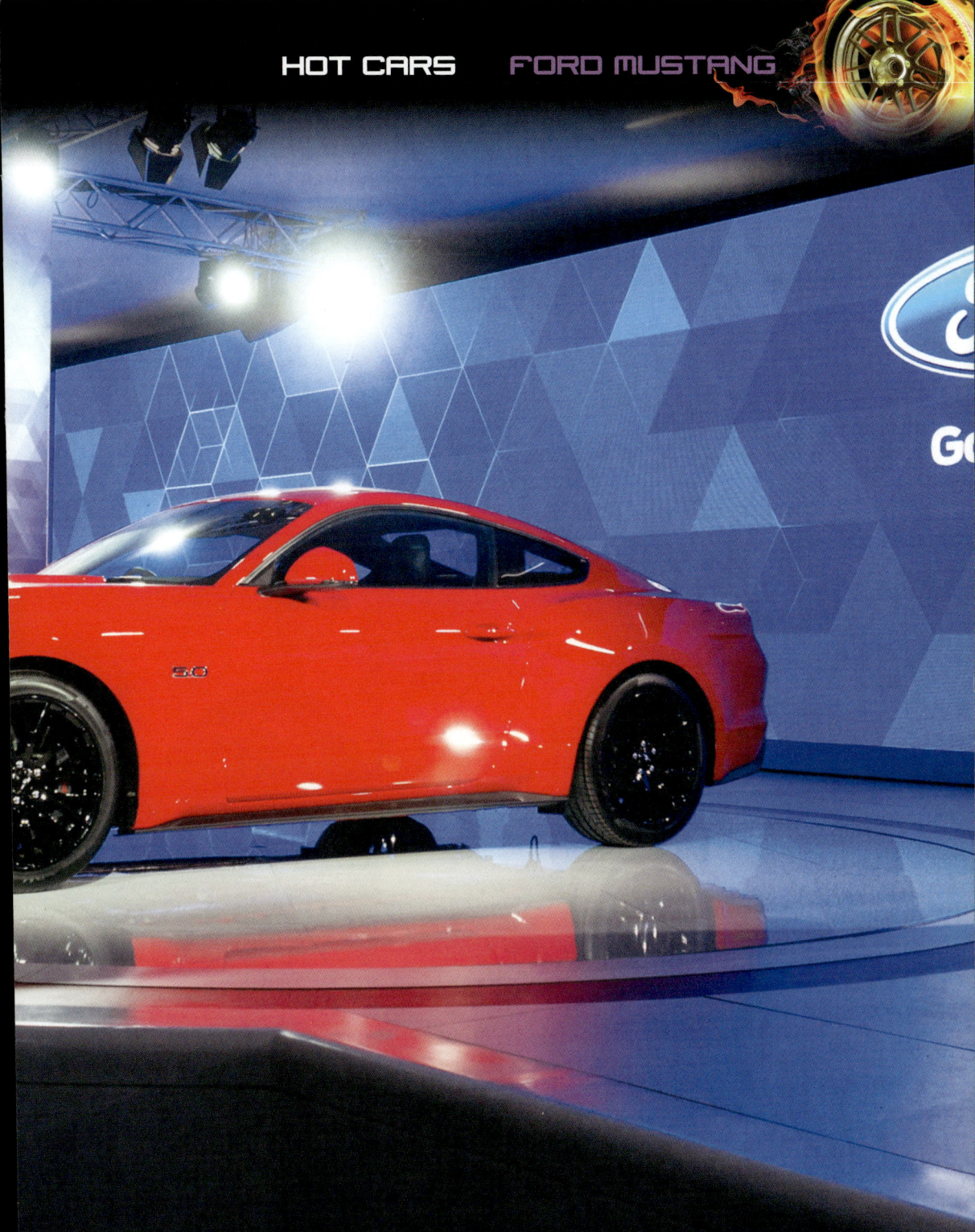

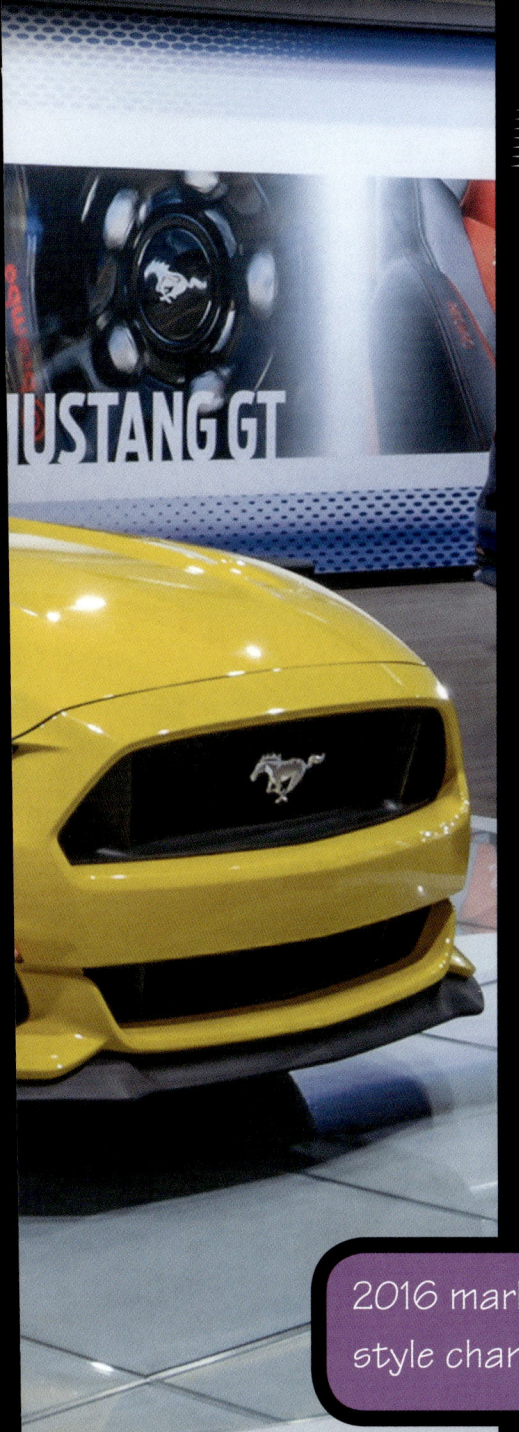

NEW LOOK

The 2016 Mustang is designed to attack the road with power. Moray Callum, a Ford vice president, says Ford has created a new look for Mustang in 2016. "We have lowered the hood two inches (five centimeters) [to improve] the **aerodynamic** shape of the car, which increased downforce and cooling airflow."

Downforce is a wind force acting on a car having the effect of pressing the car down toward the ground. That gives the car better **stability**, especially at high speeds.

2016 marks the sixth generation of style changes to the Mustang.

American Muscle Car

Today's Mustang, like its **predecessors**, comes from a long line of muscle cars. Muscle cars were lighter, two-door cars with powerful V-8 engines. They were made for street driving and occasional drag racing.

HOT CARS   FORD MUSTANG

Most experts say the first muscle car was the 1949 Oldsmobile Rocket 88.

1949 Oldsmobile Rocket 88

HOT CARS — FORD MUSTANG

Ford has built Mustangs near its home base in Dearborn, Michigan, for 49 years.

Besides the Mustang, other famous muscle cars were the Chevy Corvette and the Dodge Charger. Many experts say the era of the muscle cars ended in 1973 when gasoline shortages and emission controls put the brakes on cars that burned a lot of gasoline. Still, the V-8 engine in today's Mustang Shelby GT350 remains a muscle car powerhouse.

The engine's code name is "Voodoo." It produces a blistering 526 horsepower and 429 pound-feet of torque. It is among the most powerful engines that Ford has produced.

HOT CARS — FORD MUSTANG

Lee Iacocca's Baby

The father of the Mustang is Lee Iacocca, a U.S. automobile executive. At Ford Motor Company, he had a vision of an American-made sports car similar to those made in Europe.

Lee Iacocca

In addition to the Mustang, Iacocca took part in the design of the Ford Pinto, Ford Escort, and the Continental Mark II.

Iacocca struggled to get the approval from Henry Ford II, the head of the Ford Motor Company, to go ahead and develop the car. But finally Ford supported the idea. Iacocca unveiled the new car at the New York World's Fair on April 13, 1964.

HOT CARS   FORD MUSTANG

The interior of the 1964 Mustang was very cool for its time.

In announcing the Mustang, he appealed to young people. "We designed the Mustang with young America in mind," he said. "We like to think that … we have succeeded in wrapping up, in one package, all the elements of what we call performance." By the weekend after Iacocca's announcement, Ford had sold 22,000 of the cars. It was a smashing success.

> Iacocca eventually became president of the Ford Motor Company, but left in 1978. He later headed up the Chrysler Corporation. He retired from Chrysler in 1992.

HOT CARS   FORD MUSTANG

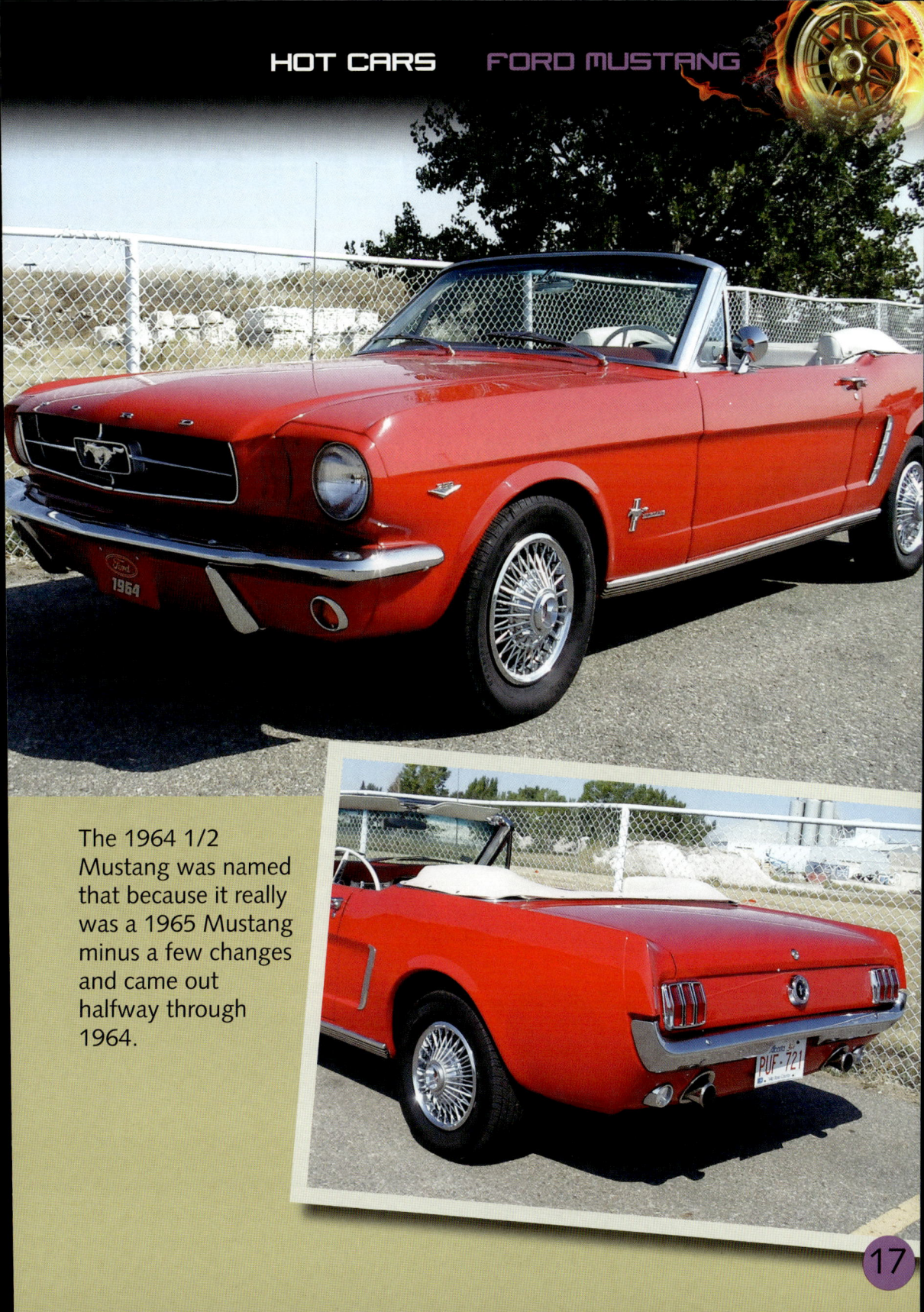

The 1964 1/2 Mustang was named that because it really was a 1965 Mustang minus a few changes and came out halfway through 1964.

A Mustang Timeline

1964 (Sept. 17): The 1965 Mustang is released. It is the most successful launch for the Ford Motor Company since the Model A was launched in 1927.

1966 (March): Sales of the Mustang pass the one million mark.

1969: Ford adds new versions of the Mustang: the Mustang Mach 1; Mustang Boss with 290 horsepower; Mustang Boss with 375 horsepower; and the Mustang Grande luxury model.

1969 Ford Mustang Boss

HOT CARS   FORD MUSTANG

1969 Ford Mustang Mach I

HOT CARS   FORD MUSTANG

1971 Ford Mustang Boss 351

1971: The largest Mustangs ever join the lineup. They are nearly a foot (30.5 centimeters) longer and 600 pounds (272.2 kilograms) heavier than earlier Mustangs.

1974: The Ford Mustang II is introduced. A complete redesign, it is nearly 500 pounds (226.8 kilograms) lighter and 19 inches (48.6 centimeters) shorter than previous models.

HOT CARS   FORD MUSTANG

1974 Ford Mustang Ghia

"The Mustang set off a revolution almost to the level of the Model T in terms of making a sports car affordable to the average person. When you were driving a Mustang, you were special. You were noticed. You stood out. And today the Mustang delivers the same **attributes**."
– Bob Witter, Ford Executive

HOT CARS   FORD MUSTANG

1984 Ford Mustang GT

1983: The Mustang convertible is back after being absent for ten years. The convertible has a power top and a tempered glass rear window.

1987: Another redesign for the Mustang is introduced. This one features a new "aero" body design.

HOT CARS   FORD MUSTANG

1987 Ford Mustang

The first known customer to buy a Mustang, Gail Brown, purchased her blue convertible from a Chicago Ford dealer. Nearly 50 years later, she still owns the car.

1990: A driver's-side airbag becomes standard for all Mustangs.

1992: The Mustang LX 5.0 outsells all other Mustang models combined.

1993 Ford Mustang 5.0 V-8 Engine

HOT CARS   FORD MUSTANG

1998 Ford Mustang

1994: In honor of its 30th anniversary, the Mustang gets a makeover. Of the vehicle's 1,850 parts, 1,330 of them are changed.

1998: The Mustang GT's V-8 engine is improved and increased to 225 horsepower.

1999: The Mustang receives another makeover, including a new hood, grille, lights, wheel arches, and sharper lines.

HOT CARS   FORD MUSTANG

2006 Ford Mustang Boss

2006: An instrument panel featuring 125 different colored lights is offered, an industry first. Mustang GT models now include 18-inch (45.7 centimeter) wheels.

2008: A farmer in Iowa buys the nine millionth Mustang, a GT convertible.

In 2007 Ford introduced a special "Warriors in Pink" Mustang, designed to help raise funds for the Susan G. Komen breast cancer foundation.

HOT CARS   FORD MUSTANG

2010 Ford Mustang

2010: The Mustang is restyled with a more muscular design.

2014 (April 16 – 17): Ford celebrates its 50th anniversary by displaying the 2015 Mustang convertible on the observation deck of the Empire State Building in New York City. New York is where the first Mustang made its **debut** during the 1964 World's Fair. The car was cut into pieces in order to be transported by elevator to the top of the Empire State Building. It was then reassembled.

Lights, Camera, Mustang!

It didn't take long for the Mustang to break into the movies. Mustang's movie career began in 1964, in the James Bond film *Goldfinger*. In 1968, in the movie *Bullitt*, Steve McQueen is a police detective who drives a Mustang GT390 in a nine-minute, 42-second car chase in San Francisco.

In all, Mustangs have been featured in more than 500 movies, including *The Bucket List* (2007) and *Race to Witch Mountain* (2009), starring Dwayne "The Rock" Johnson.

In addition to movies, hundreds of songs have been written mentioning Mustangs, beginning with "Mustang Sally" by Wilson Pickett in 1967.

HOT CARS   FORD MUSTANG

Getting Greener

The 2016 Ford Mustang has a more stylish design. It has a more powerful motor, new wheels, and optional racing stripes. But what about the years to come? Ford says it will try to make the legendary muscle car "greener." The company is looking into producing hybrid versions of the Mustang and even an all-electric version.

A man in Texas has converted his 1968 Mustang into an 800 horsepower all-electric car that can go from zero to 60 miles (96.6 kilometers) per hour in three seconds.

GLOSSARY

aerodynamic (air-oh-dye-NAM-ik): designed to move through the air very easily and quickly

attributes (AT-ruh-byoots): qualities or characteristics that belong to or describe something

debut (DAY-byoo): a first public appearance

essence (ES-uhns): the most important quality of something that makes it what it is

predecessors (PRED-uh-ses-urs): things that came before

stability (stuh-BIL-i-tee): the quality of being firm and steady

torque (tork): a measure of the turning force on car wheels

INDEX

airbag   24
Callum, Moray   9
downforce   9
Empire State Building   27
Iacocca, Lee   6, 14, 15, 16
Model A   18
Model T   21
muscle cars   10, 11, 13
Mustang (horse)   4, 6,
Mustang (plane)   4, 5, 6,
Mustang movies   28
Mustang songs   28
New York World's Fair   15
Witter, Bob   21

SHOW WHAT YOU KNOW

1. What language does the word *Mustang* originally come from?
2. What does torque measure?
3. What are the characteristics of muscle cars?
4. Who is the man mainly responsible for developing the Mustang?
5. What is the connection between the actor Steve McQueen and the Mustang?

WEBSITES TO VISIT

www.edmunds.com/ford/mustang/history
www.history.com/this-day-in-history/ford-mustang-debuts-at-worlds-fair
www.caranddriver.com/features/ford-mustang-through-the-years-a-retrospective

ABOUT THE AUTHOR

Charles Piddock is the former Editor-in-Chief of Weekly Reader Corporation. He has written many books for both young people and adults. He and his wife live by a lake in south-central Maine.

Meet The Author!
www.meetREMauthors.com

© 2017 Rourke Educational Media

All rights reserved. No part of this book may be reproduced or utilized in any form or by any means, electronic or mechanical including photocopying, recording, or by any information storage and retrieval system without permission in writing from the publisher.

www.rourkeeducationalmedia.com

PHOTO CREDITS: Cover courtesy of Ford Motor Company; pages 14-15 © Sicnag, page 16 interior shot © Jonathan Stonehouse, page 17 © dave_7 from Lethbridge, Canada; page 19 bottom photo © jeremyg3030, page 25 © Drinkingpark; page 21 source https://www.flickr.com/photos/42220226@N07/14389802775 © Sicnag; page 22 source https://www.flickr.com/photos/52900873@N07/14692032751 © Greg Gjerdingen
Images from Shutterstock.com: Header art © Petrosg; speedometer art © didis; pages 2-3 © Kurmyshov; pages 4-5 horse © Anaite; page 6 logo © diamant24; page 10-11 © DeepGreen; page 13 engine © Sergey Kohl; page 14 Lee Iacocca © Featureflash Photo Agency
Images from Dreamstime.com: pages 6-7 car shot © Amlan Mathur; pages 8-9 © Steve Lagreca; pages 12-13 © Steve Lagreca; page 18 g © Sigurbjorn Ragnarsson, page 19 Mustang Boss and page 20 © Raytags; page 23 and page 24 © Kathryn Sidenstricker, page 26 © Johann Ragnarsson, page 27 © Piotr Wawrzyniuk

Edited by: Keli Sipperley

Cover design by: Rhea Magaro
Interior design by: Nicola Stratford   www.nicolastratford.com

Library of Congress PCN Data

Ford Mustang / Charles Piddock
 (VROOM! Hot Cars)
 ISBN 978-1-68191-747-4 (hard cover)
 ISBN 978-1-68191-848-8 (soft cover)
 ISBN 978-1-68191-939-3 (e-Book)
Library of Congress Control Number: 2016932710

Rourke Educational Media
Printed in the United States of America, North Mankato, Minnesota

Also Available as: